Chapter 1

"If I have another blind date like that I swear I'm becoming a nun, Angela. He literally asked me to send him a pic while we were in the middle of eating appetizers. He could have at least waited until he paid the check!" Angela, of course, laughs at me while we are facetiming because she was the one who set this date from hell up. "Well at least he paid the check, the last one dined and dashed on you," Angela replied with a smug grin on her face that made me want to jump right through my phone and strangle her. S/N, I should pitch that idea to Apple for a future upgrade. Anyways, I quickly ended the call with her and put on my pajamas. All the money I spent on getting super cute just to end up alone back at my apartment with my cat Simba. Story of my life.

My name is Noelle Jones. 29, ad executive, and future CEO of a fortune 500 company. I am one of the youngest in my position and the only sista as well. My professional life couldn't be any better right now. Unfortunately, with all that I have in my career, I more than lack in my love life. I am a hopeless romantic. I grew up reading the fairy tales about prince charming and knew one day I wanted that for myself. I also grew up wearing thrift store hand-me-downs and living off government assistance so having success and money definitely took precedence over love. I have always been an overachiever. Valedictorian of my high school. Graduated top of my class in college, blah blah blah. Climbed the ranks from an intern to where I am today. Yet, the only love I'm getting at night is cuddles from my 3-year-old gray and black tabby I broke down and adopted because talking to myself at night made me feel just a tad bit crazy.

"I think I'm going to break down and sign up for online dating, Simba, what's the worst that can happen?" all he did was look at me sideways with those judgey eyes like he always does. SinglePeopleMeet.com is the leading online dating site. If I can't find a decent guy on there, I might as well give up trying.

Name? Noelle Jones... Age? 28... 29, let me just be honest. Height? 5'6". Weight? 160. "I can round down, Simba, don't look at me like that!" he's judging me again, but I don't care. These questions are a bit too personal anyway. Ok. I'm done with my bio. It probably shouldn't be six paragraphs long, but I want them to know what they are getting into. As an ad exec, I know how to sell myself. That just sounded terrible, but you know what I mean. Ok. Now to choose the best picture. I want something that says I'm successful and independent but I want a man to love me and I'm sexy. This pic in my cute teal tailored shirt should do it. I have one button too many unbuttoned, just enough to show a little off but still tasteful. Ok, upload and done. Hopefully tomorrow morning I'll have a thousand replies, and I can get married already. Goodnight, Simba. I have to look well rested for Mr. Right.

    7:15am and I'm already heading out the door. My condo is 5 miles from my job, and I'm like 10 minutes away even in the worst traffic, but the early bird catches the worm, and the early executive gets promoted while her competition is probably just waking up. Angela is already at Starbucks getting our skinny latte with soy milk that we religiously drink every day. I'm not a nice person in the morning unless I have my coffee and since I'm kissing a little butt to get this promotion, I need to have my best foot forward.

"Hey girl!" Angela shouts to me as she walks quickly through the company lobby, holding our coffee. She's this tiny Latino lady. Couldn't be any taller than 5 feet, and that's in heels, and weighs 110lbs soaking wet, but you can hear her from a mile away. She sounds like Sophia Vergara's more ethnic sister. "Hey, Angela, and everyone else in the building that heard you yell at me!" I replied sarcastically. Angela is my secretary, but we had formed a tight bond over the years, and now I consider her to be my closest friend. She is beautiful and brilliant. Soon as she finishes her master's degree, I hope she can take my position, after I become CEO of course. She has the home life I would love to have. A husband that worships the ground she walks on, two adorable kids, and the white picket fence around her cute suburban house. I had her set me up on a couple of blind dates with her husband's friends and colleagues and let's just say, birds of a feather don't always flock together.

"Did you remember to email me the notes for today's presentation?" I asked her. "Of course Noelle, I'm loud, not slow!" she replied and rolled her eyes at me. That's the type of relationship we have. Sarcastic and feisty. Just the way I like it.

"Don't laugh at me, but I signed up for Singlepeoplemeet.com last night," I told her hoping she didn't give me the same judgmental look Simba did, but she didn't. She actually said to me, "finally, you listened to me. You know that's the way I met my Eddy!" I knew she met her husband online, but it just wasn't on track with that fairy tale idea I had of meeting my prince. We talked for a bit more, and then I went into my office to check my emails and review the notes for today's presentation.

Well, it's 45 minutes until I actually have some work to do. My coffee is gone, and I hate being bored. I basically have all my notes memorized, so I need to find something to do. I know, let's see if my future husband has fallen in love with my profile. Ugly, too old, too creepy, just ewww, what kind of website is this? All the creeps are hitting me up. Wait. Hmmm, he's yummy...32, lives in England, beautiful blue eyes, Daniel Seymour, wait, is that THE Daniel Seymour? Son of Richard Seymour, the old inventor with even older money? This has to be too good to be true. These people are billionaires. Why would he want to talk to a kinky hair chick like myself? Don't get me wrong, I'm hot. My body is snatched, and I look barely over 21, but I don't know if I'm billionaire hot. Well, he did send me a message saying how simply gorgeous I am. Let me just respond. Harmless conversation with a little catfish digging will definitely give me something to do.

"Hello, Daniel. I am flattered that you find me so attractive. I find you attractive as well. Can I ask, out of all the women on that side of the pond, what makes you want to talk to a girl from Atlanta, Georgia?" and send. Hopefully, that wasn't too forward, but I need to know if this is something I need to call Niv and Max for. Let me get to my meeting and check back with McDreamy later.

Chapter 2

"I miss you too, Daniel! I can't wait to get off and call you so I can hear that sexy accent of yours lol" I pushed send and put my phone away. He is such a distraction. A much-needed distraction, but a distraction nevertheless. We have been talking non-stop since the day he responded to my profile. Seven wonderful months of communicating with someone other than my cat. I know I took a huge risk talking to someone online, but I checked everything out. It is actually him. We've facetimed several times. Some even undressed but that's TMI. My life seems way too perfect right now. Landed the promotion. Got Angela a promotion, and dare I say it? I've fallen in love. The absolute best part about it all is my job is requiring that I go to England for one year and head the international department of the company! I'm so excited I can just scream. I get to finally see my love in person. He can't travel here because a minor altercation with a jealous asshole got him 18 months of house arrest at his parent's mansion, but who wouldn't want to visit England and stay in a multi-million dollar estate?

"I'm going to miss you, Angie!" I was fighting back tears giving my best friend one last hug before I boarded the private jet. "We are going to facetime every day, Noelle, and as soon as I can visit you know we are coming to put some Latin flare in that stuffy country." I felt a single tear run down her cheek and onto mine. I love her so much. We let go, and I boarded my plane. I never thought I would be CEO and flying in a private jet. Not bad for a poor kid from the ghetto. Everything feels so surreal. I was sad to leave everything behind but excited to be headed to my future. Today is the day I meet my love for the first time in person. Today is the first day of my forever.

Jetlagged isn't a strong enough word to describe how I felt. Before today the furthest I've ever flown was to Miami for spring break and let's just say it was a couple year's ago. It smells different here. Like old history and dreams. I was excited about arriving but exhausted. I didn't want Daniel to see me like that, so I booked a hotel room at the airport to shower…nap…and redo my makeup. I wanted to make a great first impression. After I got dressed, I waited nervously for my car to arrive. He ordered a limo to pick me up and take me to the estate. I wondered what he would say. I wondered what I would say. Would he think I was as gorgeous in person as he always told me I was? Would his parents look past my ethnic exterior and see me as he does? I had to calm myself down because I started to sweat and that definitely isn't a good first impression.

As we pulled up to the estate, it felt as though the driveway went on for miles. It was so beautiful and secluded like it was its own little country. I've never seen a house this big in person. Not even the Whitehouse could compare to the colossal building rapidly approaching up ahead. The driver put the car in park, Got out, and opened my door. My heart skipped a beat, and my knees felt weak. "pull it together girl!" I said to myself as I pulled my charcoal gray pencil skirt down and adjusted my lilac top. I wanted to look professional yet beautiful. Modern yet timeless. I wanted to be the girl you would bring home to meet your parents but would fondle under the table. My cute pointed toe black strappy sandals were the perfect shoe to accentuate my long legs, and since he was an ass man, my pencil skirt tastefully showed all I had to offer.

As I walked to the door, I could feel my heart pounding. I rang the bell and heard its melody chime throughout the house. The echo seemed to go on forever. Just as I thought I couldn't hold myself up any longer, the door opened up. Standing before me was Daniel. He was beautiful. 6 feet tall...Muscular...chiseled jaw line...dark chocolate hair and eyes bluer than the bluest ocean. I nearly melted or at least made a puddle. Before I could open my mouth to speak which I'm sure would have sounded like a bumbling fool he took me into his arms and kisses me deeply. I felt the whole world disappear and in that second only the two of us existed. I was hooked. I knew in that second I never wanted to kiss another man again.

"Let the girl come up for air!" I heard a deep voice say from behind Daniel. It was his father. He had snuck up on us while we were so entangled in each other's arms that we didn't even hear him approaching. "Delightful to meet the girl who's stolen my boy's heart." He said in a pleasant voice. "The honor is all mine" I managed to say while adjusting my clothes once again. His father looked so different from him. He was tall but so thin. He had salt and pepper hair and hazel eyes. I figured he must take after his mother. Nevertheless, he had a pleasant and inviting disposition. I felt welcomed. "Come my dear let me introduce you to my wife" he stated. He grabbed my hand, instructed the butler to put my things away, and led me to the kitchen. Daniel following close behind.

"Honey... this is the famous Noelle Jones that has stolen our son's heart from us," Richard said jokingly. I walked over to the kitchen island to shake his mother's hand. "I'm so happy to finally meet you" I managed to say in the most meek voice I think I've ever used. "Likewise," she said in an unimpressed tone and a distinct English accent. Boy if looks could kill, I'd probably would be pronounced dead at the scene. She looked at me as if her arch nemesis walked through the door. She shook my hand anyway, probably because she was a proper lady and would not stoop down enough to be blatantly rude. "How was your flight in from... where is it? Alabama?" She asked in the most belittling voice. " Actually, it is Atlanta, Georgia, and it was just fine. The private jet was very accommodating" I said in a condescending way. This old bird really just tried to downplay my whole life with that comment. I might not be a billionaire, and my skin may be a few shades too dark for her taste but, I am a self-made woman and a very successful one at that. I will not be intimidated by some wrinkled old lady with white hair and more years behind her than ahead.

"Well dear, I would certainly hope they would be. I heard you had a recent promotion to CEO of international affairs. The least they could do was provide a simple jet" she said with a smirk on her face. I've never thought about hitting an elderly person until today. She was not going to be as easy as his dad. My looks alone were enough to win him over. I have to win her over with charm and intelligence. Luckily, that is my strong suit.

    I retreated from the conversation with scary Mary and took Richard up on his offer to do a grand tour. It would provide me enough of a distraction to forget how insulting she was, and enough time to prepare for our next meeting at dinner. She said she prepared her version of "soul food" so that I would feel right at home. Once again I almost smacked her, but since I'd be staying here with Daniel for the duration of his house arrest, I'm guessing that might be frowned upon. Daniel agreed to accompany me on the tour. We held hands as we walked the big ornate hallways and everything felt right with the world. Oil Paintings of grandparents and great grandparents adorned the walls. Gold leafing and crown molding were everywhere. It looked like Michelangelo himself painted the murals on the ceilings. This place was fit for royalty.

"This is our library. We have some of the oldest literature ever written right on these shelves" he boasted. I could tell he was very proud of all of his many possessions. "next stop on the tour is the family theater." We took an elevator down one flight, and I stepped into a room that would put any playhouse to shame. He had a projector screen about half the length of a football field that raised into the ceiling and revealed a large stage for plays and musicals. "We had the orchestra the performed at princess Diana's funeral here last Christmas." "This year we are considering a Play" These people had money to blow. I have never seen so many "things" in one place. Statues from Greece. Samurai swords from China. Ancient artifacts from

Africa that Scary Mary said I absolutely had to see. Did I mention how much I want to hit her? Anyways we walked for what felt like an hour and finally ended the tour at a private door.

"Noelle you are welcome to any place in my home. The pool, the theater, the library, the gardens. I want you to feel as comfortable as possible. All that I ask is that you never go past this door. I have some top secret inventions that I am working on that not even my wife is allowed to see. If you can promise me that, I'd love for you to stay as long as you'd like!"

It seemed a little creepy for him to be so serious about the secret wing of the house but I agreed. Most rich people are a bit eccentric. Combine that with being a world renown inventor and married to Scary Mary for 45 years and it made perfect sense.

He left us to take his daily nap, and finally Daniel and I were all alone. He was so beautiful. Every inch of that man was perfect. He picked me up in his arms and carried to his room. his arms felt so powerful. His room was big enough to fit my whole condo in it. That's not even counting his master bathroom and fitness room. He laid me on his bed gently and began gazing into my eyes.

"Words cannot describe the joy I feel to have you here with me," he said. "You are even more ravishing in person." His accent was so sexy. I felt myself throb a bit, but after all, it had been over a year since I've been this close to any man. "You are the sexiest man I've ever met," I said to him in my seductive voice. "This is the happiest day of my life" It really was. Despite the not so welcome introduction to his mother, I was on cloud 9. Everything I ever wanted I had. It took us all of our will power not to rip off each other's clothes right then and there, but we had dinner in an hour, and I wanted to take my time with him. I wanted to get to know every inch of him, paying special attention to about 8 of those inches, and I know he wanted to do the same. He just kissed me passionately. Like my lips were the sweetest piece of fruit he has ever had. I felt him grow against my thigh. I ached for him too. It was hot enough to start a fire in that room.

Chapter 3

"What about this one Angela? It's elegant yet sexy" I face-timed her to get her input on my dinner attire. Scary Mary asked me to put on something more appropriate for dinner. Just another jab at me to add to the list. "That's a little too slutty," said Angela. "Ooh, what about the black little number we bout from Saks before you left?" "That's perfect!" I said. Angela always knew what would look great on me. I put the dress on right on camera. We were close like that. "See, you look awesome. Let's see Bloody Mary say anything about this one," she said. "It's Scary Mary Angela, and I'm sure she'll find something to say." Daniel and I were getting a bit too hot, so he decided to go take a dip in the pool. That was just what I needed because I had to call Angela and tell her all about him plus check on my first love Simba. She was kind enough to take him in until I figured out whether they were cat people. I pinned up my coiled tresses into a neat high bun. I wanted to look neat and sophisticated instead of the wild child I showed up as, with my hair blowing freely in the Autumn air. "Don't forget Simba only eats organic chicken beef or fish. None of that canned food. I just deposited five hundred dollars in your account so that should be enough to cover his expenses until I talk to Daniel about his competition. If you need any extra, please let me know" I know. He's spoiled. In my defense, he was the only living thing I had to spoil other than myself. So why not splurge on my love. "Girl I know. Not meow mix, no cheap litter, and all the cat trees his little heart can desire. Simba is in great hands. You just worry about Scary Mary and the secret wing of the house." She was right. I knew Simba would be just fine. I took him on play dates with her kids to make sure they would get along. Please don't judge me for that either. My issue was impressing his mother so she'd give me her blessing to stay as well. "Okay, Angie I'll call you tomorrow night and give you the 411 on my dinner and my dessert aka Daniel. Kiss Simba for me please!" We ended the call, and I put on my black louboutin pumps and my Tiffany bracelet. I wanted to show I had a little money of my own. I took a deep breath and walked the long hallways to the formal dining room.

"Wow! You look simply beautiful!" Daniel said to me as I entered the room. "How is it that you get more beautiful each time I see you?" I blushed as he pushed me up to the table next to him. "Yes dear you do clean up well" His mother actually paid me a compliment. At that moment I felt more at ease than I did the whole trip. "Thank you, Mrs. Seymour," I said. "Please dear, call me Mary. I am still young at heart" she replied. "Okay then Mary. Thank you for making this wonderful meal for me. You didn't have to go through so much trouble for me" I said trying to sound extra appreciative. "It's no trouble at all. I've cooked for my husband for the last 45 years every single night. It's part of being a good wife. I don't suppose you cook much being a modern woman on the go and CEO?" If I didn't know any better, I'd think that could be a compliment, however, I know better and she's just insulting me again in her ever so proper way. "Actually I was taught how to cook by my mother before she passed away. I specialize in southern cuisine, and I can't wait to taste your version of it" I said with a smirk on my face. I shut her up and let her know she's the one being judged now. I don't know who taught her how to fry chicken anyways she's as English as they come. She probably watched Paula Dean reruns to perfect her craft. "Mom Noelle was telling me how much she adores your decorating skills," Daniel said interrupting the awkward silence in the room. I love the way he was trying to make his mom take a liking to me. He really wanted me to be comfortable here with him, and he knew it would be close to impossible if his mom kept treating me like the enemy.

"Well thank you, Noelle. Everything in this house was decorated by me except Richard's study, His man cave, and of course his private wing he built onto the house. I never even got to see the floor plans for it" she said to me in a very irritated voice. "Don't start dear. You just said you had complete control over almost everything. Let me have my private wing and my other rooms please!" He said sounding equally irritated by his wife. I could tell he was controlling, but she was unbearable. I couldn't imagine how they managed to make it 45 years but, they seem to really love each other.

"Ah...here's supper," said Daniel at the perfect moment. He was great like that. Always knowing what to say at the right time. The servers all came filing out of the kitchen with silver trays of food. Although she cooked it, Scary Mary still wanted to be waited on hand and foot. The food smelled delicious. Fried chicken, macaroni and cheese, collard greens, yams, deviled eggs, cornbread, and a pitcher of sweet tea and lemonade. I was amazed at how great everything looked. "You have certainly outdone yourself," I said, trying to not sound as shocked as I was. "Thank you, dear. I learned out to cook from my mother's housekeeper big mama. I just love soul food." She looked so proud of herself. She should be, it was delicious.

After dinner, Daniel and his father went to his study for a scotch and a cigar to give me and Mary some "alone time". The conversation throughout dinner was surprisingly pleasant, and she wanted to continue over a glass of wine. She brought out an expensive bottle that was older than I am and had her butler pour it for us in some beautiful crystal glasses. "Noelle, I'm very pleased with how knowledgeable you seem to be on so many different topics. No wonder my son is so taken by you. I know I can be a bit difficult at times but Daniel is my only child, and I have to protect him. As you can understand a man of his wealth and stature can be victim to a girl trying to make something of herself. I want to make sure he is loved for who he is and not what he has." At that moment it all made sense to me. She was right. Daniel is rich and beautiful. He stands to gain billions from his inheritance, and if that were my child, I would be on edge too. "Mrs. Seymour...I mean Mary, I love your son. I spent my whole life building this career for myself and yet your son is by far the best thing that has ever happened to me. He completes me and makes me a better person. I know I make him better too. It would give me no greater pleasure to spend the rest of my life with him. I'd like to gain a mom and dad with that too. I lost both of my parents some time ago. Daniel is truly blessed to have you both." It was at that moment her face softened up. I could see the beauty and love in her eyes that seemed to be sparkling from the tears she held back as I spoke. "That's all I wanted to hear," she said. "Please, stay here as long as you'd like" I couldn't help myself. I grabbed her up and gave her a great big hug. I could tell she was caught off guard, but a few seconds later she squeezed me back and smiled at me. We finished our wine and retired to our bedrooms shortly after.

I showered and put my sweet smelling lotion on every part of my body. I wanted to smell as good as I looked. It took me one month to find the perfect lingerie to wear for my first night with Daniel. It was a silk pink little number that barely covered anything. I worked off that great meal before I showered because I wanted to look perfect for him. I let my hair down and lit some candles all around. I put on that baby making music my mom used to listen to soft and low in the background. Isley Brother's greatest hits was going to be the soundtrack of our love making. I texted him to come keep me warm. He had already showered in the other bathroom after his night run around the track they have on the property. He has got to be the luckiest man alive to be on house arrest. Everything he could ever need was either already there or would be provided for him. Money was no object. My thoughts got interrupted by the sound of the doorknob turning. I struck a sexy pose as he opened the door.

"Wow! You look good enough to eat" with a smirk that made me shiver. His already sexy voice was lower than usual. It's the way he talks to me whenever we had video sex When I was in the states. He walked up to me and kissed me deeply. His hands exploring my body like he was trying to get to know every part of me. He ran his fingers through my hair. Then down my back. He grabbed my ass firmly and squeezed it. He let out a low moan, and I felt him grow up against me. My whole body felt euphoric. Just him caressing and kissing me was almost enough to bring me to orgasm. My pussy throbbing and wet from excitement. He picked me up, and I wrapped my legs around his body. He walked me to the bed, but this time he threw me down. He took my thong off first. Making sure to caress my lips with his fingers. I moaned loudly from the pleasure and anticipation. He kissed my toes and worked his way up my thighs. Each lick feeling like lightening. He kissed all around it. Inner thigh, stomach, even the outer lips. His teasing was agonizing yet delightful. Just when I thought I would go mad from longing for him, he dove in face first, devouring me as though he hadn't eaten in weeks. He licked and sucked and kissed me over and over. I never in my life have been tasted this way. I felt a wave flow from my toes and rush up my body. I climaxed harder than I ever have. I moaned so loud I swear the whole estate hear me. I didn't care. I shook and clenched the sheets as the wave of pleasure died down. He stood up and removed his boxer briefs. Revealing all that he had to offer. It was thick and long. Bigger than I expected it to be because the videos and pictures did it no justice…I scooted to the end of the bed and took him into my mouth. He let out a low groan that vibrated my soul. I began sucking and licking him. Up and down. Deep-throating every inch of him. I practiced not gagging with popsicles just for this very moment. I wanted every inch of him. I licked his testicles while rubbing his shaft then switched and kept sucking. His legs started to shake as he pulled my hair and guided my head. He let out his nectar all in my mouth. He tried to pull away, but I took him in deeper. Swallowing every single drop. Mama don't play no games, and I clean up my messes. When I finished, he just stood there staring at me. He had the look of utter disbelief on his face. I knew I had him, and he had me too. He climbed on top of me still hard and threw my legs over his shoulders. He slid inside of me slowly and deep. I let out a gasp of air. He felt so good inside of me. He slid in and out while working his hips in a swivel pattern. Baby had rhythm. Deeper and deeper he went. Wetter and wetter I got. He kissed me softly and whispered how good it was in my ear. "You feel so good baby, you're s damn wet. I love you so much" he said to me over and over. My moans were loud, and my breathing was shaky. This was the best sex I had ever had. This was the greatest love I ever felt. I climaxed again as he climaxed too. He didn't come out of me though. He just laid on top of me breathing heavily. We were too weak to move. Footsteps in the Dark softly playing in the background.

I'm a creep. I've been staring at him sleep for the last hour. My early bird schedule had me up at 6am despite the very long night we had. I thought I'd be tired, but I never felt more alert. Last night he did for me what no man ever has. He made love to my soul. We climaxed repeatedly to the point of exhaustion and dehydration. Then we just laid in each other's arms and talked. We laughed and talked about everything and nothing at all. From favorite childhood games to what we would name our children. He likes Daniel the second and Esther. He definitely won't be naming our daughter. Wow, I'm actually thinking about the future with someone. This is so surreal.

"How was your night?" asked Richard. I was trying to figure out if he heard us last night or if he genuinely wanted to know. "It was very nice," I said trying not to sound uneasy. "That's great Noelle. I'm glad the two of you are happy." He said with a huge grin on his face. Once again I was unsure if he was genuine or not so I decided to change the subject. "You're up early Richard. I'm glad I'm not the only early riser" "I'm always up. My ideas have no sense of time" he said. Sounding both proud and unhappy. "Well, I've decided to go for a swim and take a walk in the gardens this morning. Can you let Daniel know I'll be outside just in case he can't walk that far from the house?" He agreed, and I walked off quickly still unsure if my moans traveled far enough to be heard.

The pool is amazing. The water is the perfect temperature, and the hot tub after helped to soothe my aching muscles. It's been a while since I've bent my body in that fashion. I decided to take a walk through the gardens. Their backyard looked like a national park. Streams with fish. Rose bushes. Fruit trees. Butterflies. A piece of paradise right behind their house. I picked a bouquet of wildflowers to bring in the house. I thought it would be a nice gesture for not so scary Mary. I'm going to really like it here. I just know it. I ended my walk and proceeded back to the house. Time to put these in water and wake up my man. I loved the sound of that. Almost as nice as Noelle Seymour.

Chapter 4

These 3 weeks here have flown right by. It's almost time for me to go back to work, but I couldn't imagine leaving him for more than a couple of hours. We've spent every day together, and it's been pure magic. Richard has already started calling me his daughter and Mary has only taken a couple of jabs towards me since our heart to heart. We've made love every single night since the first. I swear each time has gotten better and better. The only negative thing is the way the workers act towards me. It's like they aren't used to someone actually speaking to them. They either ignore me completely. Find a way to speak and run off, or tell me that I probably shouldn't stay here. It gives me the creeps, but I think they just don't want another mouth to feed or another mess to clean. I can understand that. Also, my nosey personality just won't stop wondering about what's behind the door to the secret wing. It's like because it's forbidden, it's tempting me to have a peek. One time I was walking past it and I swear I heard another voice coming from back there. I was a bit tipsy from all the wine I had been drinking, but I'm almost certain.

"Baby, I can't wait until you can take off that silly ankle bracelet and you can give me a tour of your country. I've been here 3 weeks, and I've only seen your property. I'm getting a little cabin fever." I was starting to lose my mind not going anywhere but being with Daniel helped to make it more bearable. Plus if I had cabin fever I could only imagine how he felt. "I know love. Once this thing is off me, we can go anywhere you like. Not just the country but anywhere in the world. I want to give you whatever your heart desires." He knew exactly what to say to make me melt. The best part is I think he really means it too. Just then Simba jumped up on the bed and made a spot for himself right between us. He had arrived first class 4 days ago, and you'd think he knew

Daniel his whole life. We already had a perfect little family together.

"Well, I'm going to take a trip into town and get a few things. Do you need anything while I'm out?" I asked Daniel as I put on my jacket and Nikes. "No I have all that I need right here," he said as he gazed at me so lovingly. I gave him a kiss and headed to the door. "Before you leave I just want to let you know that the locals don't really care for my family. They are jealous of our wealth and makeup lies to make us look bad. It comes with the territory. Don't pay them any mind" he said with a concerned look on his face. This was the first time I've ever actually seen him look worried. What could anyone possibly say that would be bad enough to worry him so? I nodded my head and told him everything would be fine. I then got in the chauffeured SUV and told him to take me into the city.

"It's so different here Angela," I said as I walked through the market. It was a bunch of outdoor stands selling everything under the sun. I decided to face time her and let her see for herself. I missed our daily chats over coffee and our night time gossip over wine. "I have to come visit you. You seem to be glowing Noelle. I've never seen you so beautiful" she exclaimed smiling at me approvingly. "I'm happy girl! The happiest I've been in a long time. I guess great sex and true love does work miracles" I said jokingly but meaning every word. "I'll call u from the car…I need to find the ingredients for dinner tonight. It's my turn to show out in the kitchen". We ended the call, and I went to the meat stand to see if they had ox tails for the stew I wanted to make for dinner.

"Do you happen to sell ox tails here? I want to make my boyfriend and his parents' dinner," I said to the butcher. I felt silly telling him so much information, but I just loved calling Daniel my boyfriend. I wanted to tell anyone who would be willing to listen. "Well, little lady, you are in luck. We have the best ox tails in all of England right at this shop" he said in a deep boisterous voice. "Your boyfriend and his family are certainly in for a treat. They're a little pricey but worth every pound" he said as he started packaging up the meat for me. "I'll take 10lbs please…and the cost isn't important we can manage," I said trying not to sound like I'm bragging. "10lbs huh? You must do alright for yourself" he said seeming surprised at my large order. I guess he wasn't used to someone that looks like me paying so much for some meat. I decided to brag a little since he made that comment. "Well, I am CEO of international Affairs of the new Rise Ads Inc. that just opened here. Plus my boyfriend is Daniel Seymour. Son of Richard Seymour so yes I think I'm doing ok for myself" I said in a boastful voice.

You would think I mentioned the devil the way all the color drained out his plump rugged face. He stopped what he was doing and looked me in my eyes. "You are staying at the Seymour estate?" he said in a shaky voice about 2 octaves higher than the last time he spoke. "Yes, I am…why do u seem frightened at the thought?" I asked feeling suspicious about his reaction. "It's haunted up there. People have mysteriously vanished from there, and their money made sure they were never mentioned again." He sounded downright terrified as he spoke. "Richard is a very powerful man. Be careful to stay on his good side" he said quickly bagging my Ox tails and taking my money. He nearly threw my change at me and made an excuse to leave the counter. I knew Daniel said they were hated, but it seems more like they are feared more than anything else. I handed the meat to the chauffeur and proceeded to the fresh produce stand for additional ingredients.

The whole day I spent shopping I made sure to mention I stayed with the Seymour's to as many locals as possible. I wanted to gauge their responses based on the reaction of the butcher. Most reacted the same as he did. From uneasy to terrified at the mention of their name. One older lady told me her daughter went there looking for work and never returned again. It had been 5 years since she'd heard anything from her. She felt terrible because it was her idea to send her there to help provide for her sick father's care. She asked me to ask the help if they've heard of her and if she's there to ask her to call home. I agreed and gave her a hug as she sobbed on my shoulder. I had heard enough. It was definitely time to get back to the estate.

"Daniel, why didn't you tell me that everyone was scared of your family?" I asked as I chopped up the onions, carrots, and celery. " They all seem to think its haunted here and you guys are axe murderers or something" Daniel came behind me and wrapped his arms around me. I lost my breath for a second just from his warm embrace. "Darling, I warned you about the locals. They makeup nonsense and spread it around like wildfire. Look at how celebrity gossip is so popular in the states. People love a go story" he said then began kissing my neck gently. All the concern I had faded away at that moment. He sure knew how to shut me up.

I finished cooking and went to change for dinner. I finally started thinking with my brain again instead of my Netherlands and still felt a bit uneasy. I decided I would ask Richard about the young girl that disappeared at dinner. I keep my word even to strangers.

"Everything is so delicious dear," Mary said seemingly impressed by my stew and cornbread. "You must share the recipe with me so I can make it myself." I smiled and agreed still waiting on the right moment to ask about what happened. I just went for it. "so today I went into town to get a few things and the ingredients to this stew. I was amazed how terrified everyone was at the mention of your name" I said staring at Daniel as he turned beet red. "Richard they act as if you run the town and accused you of some pretty bizarre things. Richard didn't even change his expression when he replied "If I had a dollar for everything negative that was said about me I wouldn't have had to invent anything. People talk. That's all it is…is talk. You must not get caught up in petty gossip Noelle. It's not becoming of a lady such as yourself." That was the first insult he had ever fired at me. Even Mary appeared shocked by his comment. I still had to shake it off and ask about the missing girl. "well there was just an old lady saying she sent her daughter here to find work who never returned or called again. It's been over 5 years, and she was supposed to be seeking work to send some home to her sick father. Does the name Elizabeth Stewart ring a bell?" I asked, worried about his response.

Instead, Mary chimed in before Richard could and said, " I interviewed her and turned her down for the position. She was unqualified for the job and frankly didn't seem much like she even wanted it. I wouldn't be surprised if she used the opportunity to run off. Having the responsibility of your father's care on you can be too much for a girl that young. Next time make a list, and we'll send one of our butlers for you. It's clear you've had a hectic day and don't want our reputation to cause you any more problems" I felt bad retreated from the conversation. We ate the rest of our dinner in silence.

    That night, Daniel yelled at me for the first time. He was so hurt that I questioned his parents after he told me to drop it. It took some special making up in order to get him to forgive me. There are places that will be sore on me for days. We went to bed holding each other again, and I decided not to stir the pot any further.

The next day during my morning swim I caught one of the housekeepers staring at me. Not in the usual way they all stare because I'm the only chocolate they've seen in forever but in a weird way like she wanted to get my attention. I dried off with my towel and put my robe on. Using another towel to wrap my dripping hair up. I walked to the maids quarters to see if my suspicions about her were correct.

"Hey Patricia, I saw you staring at me earlier...did you need to say anything to me?" I asked her. I made it my duty to learn everyone's name from the gardener to the butler to the maids. She looked at me with an uneasy look and said "last night at supper I heard u mention Elizabeth Stewart. She did come here 5 years ago. She didn't run away either" I was getting nervous looking at how scared she seemed to talk to me. She interrupted my thoughts by telling me, " be careful about the questions you ask here. There are some answers better left unknown and unsaid." She grabbed her duster and walked off quickly. I didn't know how to take her remark. It's as though she's implying something really did happen, but she definitely wasn't going to tell me anything else. Her job and maybe more than that depended on her silence. I couldn't take the chance of asking anyone else and the family finding out. I had just begun to feel at home here. I had to play this one carefully, but I was far from done looking into it.

Chapter 5

So glad to be back at work. Don't get me wrong I love spending time with Daniel, but I was losing my mind there. I missed being productive. I missed soy lattes while reading morning emails. I also wanted to get out of that house. My cabin fever increased my paranoia. I started feeling like the staff was trying to get me to leave, and like Richard was hiding some huge secret. Mary was being typical Mary. Hot and cold. Insulting and complimentary. The only silver lining was my Daniel. We had grown so close so quickly. I felt my heart wouldn't beat the same without him. I was head over heels in love with him, but it wasn't enough to quiet my thoughts. You know what they say; "An idle mind is the devil's playground." Time to get this brain busy again.

"Everyone turn your portfolios to page 4 and follow along," I said to my new staff as I headed our first meeting at the new company. I was killing it. That break was all I needed to come back better than ever. I outlined everything from A-Z with so much confidence. I was where I was meant to be. Doing what I was born to do.

I went to my office and looked at my schedule for the rest of the day. They gave me a very competent assistant, but she was no Angela. I didn't feel comfortable trusting my day's events to a stranger. If you can't tell by now, I'm a bit of a control freak. Suddenly my phone rang interrupting me color coding each event I had planned. It was Daniel. Even after a month and a half of living together and about 9 months of dating I still got butterflies whenever his picture came across my phone.

"Hi babe, how's the best CEO in the world doing today?" He asked smiling at me lovingly. He had video called me from in the bath tub. His body was glistening from the water. He looked damn good. "My day is great especially now that I get to talk to you" I responded. Unbuttoning my top button to expose a little cleavage. I let my hair out of my bun and shook it free. I knew that turned him on to see me do that. Some naughty secretary fantasy he had conjured up when we first started talking. "Now baby you know what that does to me," he said as he lowered the camera down to his waist. Displaying the erection he had saluting from the water. It was beautiful. I instantly got moist from the sight of it. "Can Ms. Twila come out to play?" He asked as he began stroking his pole from the bottom to the tip. Ms. Twila was the name I gave my vagina years ago. I told him about it joking with him one day, and he has been calling her that ever since.

"Daniel, you know I'm working. It's my first day I can't be masturbating in my office" I knew I was going to do it anyways, I just loved hearing him beg for it. So damn sexy. He began stroking a little faster and moaning in a deep sensual tone. I throbbed at the sound of him. I got up, locked my door, closed the blinds and told my assistant I was taking lunch. I then opened my blouse and unhooked my bra, Exposing my hard chocolate nipples. I began rubbing them and biting my bottom lip. "You like this, daddy?" I said in my come-hither voice.

"Yes I love it!" he said in a breathy voice. I could tell he was getting close to climaxing. I pulled up my skirt, Pulled down my lace panties, and spread my legs wide open. I started rubbing her, moaning from the pleasure. "Damn baby I wish you were inside me right now!" I moaned. Rubbing my pearl in a quick, circular motion. He was beating it super fast now. The veins in it engorged with blood. He was rock hard. It drove me crazy. Just then his nectar shot out like a fire hydrant. It dripped down his shaft into his curly brown hairs. I felt a tingle start from my head and rushed over my entire body. I held back my moans the best I could but still made more noise than I felt comfortable making. Daniel started laughing and said, " Hopefully the walls are soundproof" I felt instantly embarrassed, but I enjoyed every bit of it. I couldn't wait to get back home to make him pay for influencing me.

I couldn't sleep. I got off, came home, ate a quick supper, and got him back for what he did to me earlier that day. I made him tap out and sent him to bed curled up like a baby. Yet after the long and eventful day I had, I could not fall asleep. It was 1am, and I had to be up in a few hours. I decided to go make me some chamomile tea in hopes that it would do the trick.

I walked the long hallways to the kitchen. The whole house was quiet. Everyone usually is asleep by 11pm, so it was just me and the creepy paintings that seem to follow you as you walk. I filled up the teapot and placed it on the stove. While I waited, I decided to walk past the forbidden door. I knew I shouldn't, but it was like a magnet drawing me closer. I got to the door and noticed the lights were on from underneath. I placed my ear on the door to see if I could hear anything coming from inside. It sounded like classical music playing from inside. Mozart or Beethoven's symphony or something. I listened a little closer. I heard Richard talking in an angry voice. "Don't make me have to punish you again," he said. I heard what sounded like whimpering as well. I tried to make out what the other voice was saying, but just as I leaned in with all my weight, the teapot started whistling. It scared the crap out of me, and I let out a scream. I ran as fast as I could, cut off the stove, and ran back to my room. I was too scared to make any tea, and after that, it was going to take more than chamomile to calm my nerves. Something just wasn't right. I had to find out what was behind that door. Or who was behind that door. It was going to be a sleepless night.

    The next day, I had a double shot of espresso added to my usual. I literally dozed off for 45 minutes before my alarm clock went off. I got to work at my usual time. As I was reading over my emails, I felt sick to my stomach. I ran to the bathroom and puked up every drop of Starbucks I consumed. I guess my body wasn't used to so much caffeine. I washed my mouth out with some mouthwash and touched back up my makeup. I sat back down at my desk to finish my emails.

"Hey, girl how's it going?" Angela IM me as I went over today's schedule. I was early as usual, so I minimized the screen and chatted with her for a bit. "Hey Angie, I love it here. I have some of the best employees, and they all seem to really respect me. How's it back in GA?" I pressed send and waited for her reply.

" Everything is great. Love my new position. Thanks for the recommendation. Just got my heating pad on high today. How are your cramps?" she asked. Angie and I were so close that we would always get our periods at the same time. I looked at my calendar. To my shock, I was 4 days late! "OMG Angie I'm late!" I typed. Just then my phone rang. It was her face timing me. "What do you mean late?" she said in a voice that sounded more afraid than mine. "I mean I haven't started my period. Plus I just blew chunks right before you messaged me." I was terrified. I got so wrapped up in Daniel I forgot all about it. Plus, we didn't always use protection. Actually, almost never. "I might be pregnant!" I said. It sounded so foreign coming out my mouth I could almost swear it wasn't my voice. "Angie sat there staring at me as though she was looking for the right words to say. "Well Noelle you are in a new country, in a different time zone, your body just might be adjusting. Don't stress yourself out. Plus you are running a whole company so that may be stressing you out enough to be late too. Take a test and then you'll know for sure." I agreed to relax as much as possible until I took a test. Angela was right there are several reasons I might be late. Plus it was only a few days off. I told her I'd call her after I peed on the stick so we could find out together.

When I got off work, I had the driver take me to the local drug store. I grabbed 2 different test just in case one malfunctioned. I kissed Daniel when I got in the house and told him about my day. Making sure to leave out the part where I might be pregnant. I just told him that the coffee made me sick and he offered to make me homemade chicken soup and soda crackers for dinner. While he cooked, I went to a bathroom and peed on both sticks. One test would turn blue if it was positive and the other would display 2 lines. I called Angela on face time so she could be there with me once I found out. "So Noelle, what exactly are you hoping for?" she asked in a concerned voice. I hadn't even thought about that. I was so worried about what the test I didn't stop to think what I wanted the outcome to be. "well Angie I love Daniel and I know he loves me. We've been dating for almost a year, but I've only been here a month and a half. He's still on house arrest, and his dad is starting to creep me out. I know he will be the father of my kids one day, I just think it's too soon." Just then the timer went off. It was time to find out the results. Angela said, "I'm right here with you and I'll be here for you either way." I took a deep breath and walked over to the sink counter.

"It's blue! It's neon blue! I don't think I've ever seen something so blue!" I said, staring at the test in disbelief. "Check the other one to make sure!" Angela said sounding more shocked than me. "Two bright pink lines Angela! I'm pregnant!" I burst into tears at that very moment. "OMG, I'm going to be a mother! Daniel is going to be a father!" At that moment I felt my stomach drop to the floor. I was going to have to tell Daniel that he was going to be a dad. I know we discussed kids names joking around, but this was no laughing matter. "What if he gets mad and kicks me out? What if he thinks they aren't his? I'll kill him if he tries to take me on Maury!" I said to Angela, talking through my tears. "He loves you, Noelle. You know he's not going to do any of those things. These things happen for a reason. It's all in God's timing. Eddy and I were pregnant only 2 months into dating and look at us now. Everything will be fine." I felt a little better and hung up the phone. I put the pregnancy tests in a gift bag I had from a necklace Daniel bought me a month ago and decided I would give it to him over dinner. Like it or not, we had a present coming within the next nine months. "I'm going to be a mom Simba!" I said to my cat. "I'm going to be a mom!" I said to myself.

Chapter 6

My armpits were sweating. I had just showered and put on a fresh coating of deodorant, yet I was a sweaty mess. I don't think I have ever been this nervous in my whole life. I was sitting in bed waiting for Daniel to bring me the soup he had made me for dinner. Next to me in the nightstand drawer was the gift bag with the test inside. I had played it over and over again how I would tell him the news, but I was still terrified of what his reaction would be. Angela had made me feel slightly at ease on the phone, but as soon as I sat down and gave it some thought, I realized the sheer magnitude of what I was about to tell him. This could either make or break our relationship. Would he be upset? Would he want to keep it? Hell, do I even want to keep it? I know we had discussed kids before, but that was before! Before the test turned blue. Before the other test had 2 pink lines. Before I had to think about how this may affect my career. Before we could even get married. All of this just seemed like too much too soon. Just as I was about to have a nervous breakdown I heard footsteps coming closer to the bedroom door.

"Honey, Your soup is ready! I brought crackers, soda water, ginger ale, lemons, whatever you need to feel better" he said with a smile. He was so good that way. He would always know exactly what to do to make me feel better. "Now I'm no chef, but I'd like to think this soup is one of the best soups you'll ever have." He handed me my tray of food and placed a napkin on my chest to protect me from any spillage. He picked up the spoon and blew it a little with his beautiful pink lips. He brought it to my mouth, and I tasted the first spoonful. "Wow, baby, this is delicious!" I said to him. It really was. I was planning on lying even if it wasn't but it was actually the best chicken soup I've ever eaten. I grabbed the spoon and finished the bowl in 5 minutes flat. He stared at me with the most pleased look on his face as I emptied the bowl. I didn't stop there though. I ate the crackers. Drank the soda water, the ginger ale, and even sucked on the lemons. "You must have been really hungry, I can go get you some more soup if you'd like," he said to me with a look of surprise on his face. One minute I tell him I'm sick, the next minute I'm scarfing down the food like it's my first meal all year. I get nervous, and then I eat. It's a bad habit, but as nervous as I was I could probably eat the whole pot of soup. I decided that I needed to just get It out the way before I ate them out of house and home.

"Daniel, how much do you love me?" I asked him while holding his hand and looking into those big blue eyes of his. " I love you more than I've ever loved anyone or anything." He replied looking worried. I felt my palms get sweaty, but I shook it off and continued talking. " Is there anything that could happen that would make you second guess your love and commitment to me?" I asked beating around the bush for as long as I possibly could. "Not unless you tell me everything I know about you is a lie, I don't think there is anything that would waver my love for you, Noelle. You are starting to worry me though. Why don't you just tell me what it is babe? I'm sure it isn't as bad as you think." He said with a more serious look on his face. I could tell all this procrastination was actually making matters worse. I opened the nightstand drawer, pulled out the gift bag, and handed it to him. He looked at me in a confused way and opened the bag.

I closed my eyes to brace myself for his reaction. "Is this for real?" He asked. "Of course it is! As if I would actually joke around about something like this." I said with a scowl on my face. He looked at the blue test, then at the pink one. Back and forth he went from test to test as if he was trying to make sense of it all. He was silent for what felt like an eternity. "Say something Damnit! Anything at all, but I cannot take the silence!" I yelled. Louder than I wanted to, but I couldn't control my emotions nor my tone. " I'm going to be a father?" He asked as if he wanted an actual answer to the question. "Yes Daniel and I am going to be a mother" I responded, still unsure of how he was feeling. Just then he knocked the empty food tray on the floor, scooped me up in his arms, and gave me the deepest kiss he's ever given me. He jumped up after the kiss on the bed and started bouncing like a school boy. "I am going to be a daddy!" He screamed with the biggest smile on his face. I was so elated. He was happier than I've ever seen him. "Marry me, Noelle. Make me the Happiest Man on earth!" He said, with tears of joy coming down his face. I jumped up and tackled him down on the bed and climbed on top of him. " Yes! Of course I will!" I screamed, kissing him over and over again. At that very moment, I knew what I wanted. I wanted that baby. I wanted him to be the father. I wanted him to be my husband. I finally had the family I always wanted. "Of course I will get you the ring of your choice. The best one money can buy!" He said, looking at my empty ring finger, but none of that mattered. He had already given me everything I could ever ask for. We were getting married! We were having a baby!

I was going to finally be Mrs. Noelle Seymour. All we had to do was break the news to our families and friends. Just then I felt a bit of my happiness disappear. I was going to have to tell scary Mary and Weird Richard that I was carrying a Seymour heir and I was going to be marrying their son. Which means I was going to be marrying them too, and all the secrets they kept as well. I decided to worry about that another day. Today was a day of celebration. Today I get to make love to my Fiancé. I was on cloud 9, and I was not going to let anything bring me down.

    I woke up in my fiancé's arms. With our baby growing inside me. We decided that we didn't want to wait another second to share the news with his parents. I had already face timed Angela last night to tell her the news. She was so ecstatic. I couldn't tell who was happier, her or me. I wished my mom was alive to share in the experience, but I felt like her presence was there and she would be very pleased with me. I had the life that she always wanted for herself. I had the life she always wanted for me. We decided to share the news with his parents over breakfast. I was nauseated from the morning sickness, but I wanted to be a united front with Daniel, so I drank some soda water, sucked on a few lemons and sucked it up. We held hands the whole way to the dining area. Smiling like 2 high school kids in love. I never thought my love could keep growing and growing, but somehow it managed to do just that. When his parents arrived at the table, we stood up in front of them and broke the news immediately.

" Noelle and I are expecting a baby. We are also getting married!" he said, gleaming from ear to ear. His father was the first to respond.

"well that's great news son, I'm happy that you 2 have decided to tie the knot. She will make a wonderful addition to the family and the baby as well." For some reason the way he said it sent chills up my spine and not in a good way. It creeped me out. Probably due to the fact that I still was uneasy about the secret wing of the house. I still wanted to know what happened to the missing girl, and who's voice did I hear coming from the door when I listened the night I couldn't sleep. I shook it off and gave him a hug anyways. Creepy or not he was going to be my father-in-law. Mary's reaction, however, wasn't as positive as everyone else's. " Don't you kids think you are moving a bit too fast? I know you chatted for a while, but it's only been a couple of months that you 2 have been living together. Then a baby is a huge responsibility. You don't know what you are getting yourselves into" she said with a look of fear on her face. It wasn't a regular look of fear that a mom would have for her only son either. It was a look as if she saw a ghost or that something terrible was about to happen. Daniel's face looked less happy than it did before we shared the news too. It was if he saw the same ghost Mary did. Like it was a big elephant in the room, and I just couldn't see it. Nevertheless, he still held my hand tight and requested that they both respect our decision. We sat down, and breakfast was served. The only person who seemed to have an appetite was Richard. There was more to this situation than what meets the eye. It was more to this family than what meets the eye. I had to find out what was going on. I couldn't bring a baby into this world nor join in holy matrimony with a family full of secrets. I knew what had to be done. I just hoped I would be able to come up with a plan that would actually work, but wouldn't destroy our family before we even had a chance.

Chapter 7

I'm officially fat. 20 weeks pregnant and my body is no longer my own. I have weird cravings for crap I'd never eat, and I pee way too much. Despite all of these things, I am happy. We just found out we are having a girl. We want to name her Summer Rose after our favorite time of year and my grandmother. Daniel is also scheduled to end house arrest any day now. All this time cooped up in this house has made me a bit looney. I've turned into Nancy Drew looking into the case of the mysterious wing. Besides working, I've dedicated way too much time into trying to get inside. I've gone and looked up the blueprints to the estate to see if there may be a secret entrance I could get into. I've listened at the door almost every night after I put Daniel to sleep…side note, he's so simple that way. I've also talked to several more locals to see if I could find out any additional information. Angela has suggested that I seek professional help. Lately, I've been inclined to agree with her. If I could just get out this house, and go somewhere far away for a while with Daniel, I'm sure it would be all I need to get over whatever mental breakdown I must be having. I'm not saying I haven't found things that fuel my desire to uncover the truth. There are a lot of new developments that I have discovered. It's just nobody should be this obsessed with trying to find something wrong when they are the happiest they've ever been. It's like part of me is trying to sabotage what I have, but I just know something isn't right about this family.

It also doesn't help that it seems like as the day draws near to Daniel being free, the more it seems as though he has no intentions of leaving. He's set up a nursery there. With murals and furniture and a whole wardrobe full of clothes. He constantly talks about his mother helping out with the baby once I return back to work; and every time I discuss looking for our own place he finds a way to change the subject. I recently found out that he's never actually lived away from home. Even while he was in college, he still stayed with his parents. It's so weird to me that a man, as mature and brilliant as he, would choose to live under the thumb of his parents for so long. I just know for my own sanity, we were not going to be able to live there much longer.

Richard has gotten more weird too. He's more distant and less friendly. The more I pry, the more I think he knows what I'm trying to do. It's to the point where Mary talks to me more than him. The staff is still constantly warning me to leave too. In subtle ways, but the message is loud and clear. It's like the only person that truly wants me to stay there is Daniel. Work is my only distraction. I'm doing so well, and our numbers are excellent. If only my home life were as great as my work life things would be perfect. Don't get me wrong I love Daniel, and I've never been happier. I would just be happier if we could get the heck out that creepy old house.

"Ms. Jones you have a call on line one." Just then my secretary interrupted my thoughts of escaping from home and all things creepy. I picked up the phone welcoming the much-needed distraction. "Hello, love. I have a surprise for you" It was Daniel. It wasn't a distraction at all. "A surprise? I wonder what it could be?" I replied trying to sound excited to hear from him. "In 15 minutes my jeweler will arrive with a selection of rings. Pick whichever one you'd like. Money is no object. I'd love to get it for you, but I'm no good at these things. This way you'll have the perfect ring. The perfect ring for a perfect woman." Just then my heart melted the way it always does whenever he does something amazing. Here I am hoping it wasn't him calling and he goes and pulls this amazing gesture off. I don't deserve him. "OMG baby thank you so much. I can't wait to show you the one I choose. I'll model it for you later…with nothing else on" I said to him. I went from dreading going home to wanting to run home to him. Whatever we were going through we would make it past it, as long as we were together, we could get through anything. We ended the call, and my secretary escorted the jeweler into my office.

" I'll take that one," I said, sliding the ring on my finger. It was a 10 karat princess cut diamond with diamonds all around the band. It had to be worth hundreds of thousands of dollars. I almost felt guilty for picking it. There were rings that were a lot more modest, but this one made me feel the way Daniel makes me feel. Like there's a field of butterflies in my stomach. I knew it was perfect for me. I thanked the jeweler and decided to leave early for the day. I was there on my off day anyways, but I made up an excuse to come in to get away from the house. I hopped in the car and told the driver to take me home. I stared at my ring the whole way there. I was in love all over again.

When I got home, Daniel was in the kitchen preparing lunch. I had called him from the car to tell him that I was coming home to thank him properly for my beautiful ring. He prepared a lovely chicken salad for us with homemade croutons just the way I liked it. I ran up to him and gave him the longest, most passionate kiss ever. He was just so perfect. I don't know what I did to be so lucky, but I wasn't going to fight it. We took the meal up to our room and sat at the little table by the window overlooking the garden. "Daniel this is the best surprise I have ever gotten! I can't believe this rock is on my finger. It looks like the iceberg that sank Titanic!" I said to him smiling ear to ear. "Anything for my queen and mother of my child" he replied with a pleased and loving look on his face. I shoveled a few bites of food into my mouth and sipped some sparkling mineral water to wash it down. I wanted to eat some of it because he took his time and prepared it just right for me, however, what I had a taste for was him. My hormones were already on overdrive due to the baby, and that romantic gesture had me making panty puddles. I got up and faced the window. Undressing slowly to tease and tantalize him slowly. Once I was naked in my full glory, I spread my legs apart. I placed my palms flat on the glass and told him to come get it. He jumped up and was naked in 2 seconds flat. He walked up to me pressing his engorged member into my round ass. He began kissing my neck and back. Each one more stimulating than the last.

Just when I thought my knees would go weak from longing for him, he slid deep inside me. I felt like an exhibitionist making love in front of the open window while the staff tended to the garden. He was rough and unforgiving with his strokes. I could tell he was getting close to climaxing. And so was I. Right as I felt the ascension to euphoria, I saw something out the corner of my eye that caught my attention in the corner of the garden by the oak trees. It looked like William, one of the gardeners was burying something. It was wrapped in what looked to be a black trash bag, but the outline was eerie. I felt all the wonderful stimulation go away and instead I felt all the blood drain from me. I was mortified. The outline of the bag looked like a human body or something very close in shape. He was burying it, and nobody seemed to care. Nobody seemed to even notice. Right as I was about to tell Daniel to stop and take a look, he shot his nectar deep inside me and wrapped his arms tightly around my body. His breath was heavy and sporadic. He definitely put in some work, but I couldn't even focus because of what I just saw. I turned around and kissed him to ensure him he did a great job. I decided I would point out the horrific sight in the garden to him, bit when I went to look out the window again, William was gone. Now I know that I've been a little obsessed with all the weird stuff going on around here, but I was not crazy. I saw what I saw. Unfortunately, if I told Daniel, he would probably just think it was pregnancy brain like he tried to explain everything else away with. This time was going to be different. I would uncover the truth...literally. I would wait until I had the opportunity to sneak out this week and dig it up for myself and take a picture as evidence. I would get to the bottom of the secrets once and for all.

Chapter 8

2 whole days. That's how long it took Daniel to finally fall asleep before me and hard enough so that I wouldn't wake him up with the slightest movement. Seems like after I got pregnant he became extremely clingy and overprotective. It's cute most of the time, but not when I have a mystery to solve. I waited until about 1am when I knew the house would be sleep and tiptoed out to the garden. I had on my combat boots and all black clothing. If it wasn't for my baby bump, you'd think I was covert ops. I quietly went into the shed and got a shovel out. Part of me knows I'm way too pregnant to be digging up graves, but my mind wouldn't rest until I knew what was there. I walked over to where I saw William digging. I stuck the shovel in the ground and took out my first scoop of dirt. It was heavy but manageable. I kept digging. Deeper and deeper I went. I dug for what felt like hours, but truthfully only about one hour passed by. It was hard work. My back

burned from all the labor and I was nervous I might actually go into labor myself. I dug until I couldn't dig anymore and then I saw it. Just a torn black trash bag. Someone had removed whatever was inside. I know I saw something big enough to be a body, but all that's behind is a taunt to let me know they were one step ahead of me; but who? Or better yet, when? I had been watching that spot like a hawk whenever I wasn't at work. They had to see me looking out the window because why else would they dig it back up? That also means they saw us having sex, but that was the least of my worries. Someone knows that I know. Someone went through great measures to keep their secret hidden. William was too slow to think this up all by himself. He was mid-40s, but had the mental capacity of a 12-year-old. There was someone e else behind this, and I bet I know exactly who it is.

I limped back to the house, trying not to make any noise. I was in so much pain. I barely made it to the stairs when I heard noises coming from the secret wing of the house. Richard was up, and he wasn't in there alone. I heard talking coming from inside again, and it wasn't his just his voice. They were yelling. Some sort of argument was going on, and although the detective in me wanted to listen, the mom in me told me to go take a shower and rest my body. This obsession was causing me to put my baby's life at risk. Digging up empty graves and sneaking around lime some spy. It was time that I made a decision. Either we move out together once the house arrest was over, or I'm moving out alone. No matter what, I couldn't live here with our baby. Daniel had to make a choice. I limped slowly up to the bedroom, undressed, showered, and went to bed.

The next day I stayed in bed majority of the day. I was so sore from last night's excursion that it even hurt to blink. When I finally got up, I went down to the kitchen to fix me something to eat. I wasn't hungry, but knew I had to eat something for the baby. I looked in the fridge about 3 times before I decided on fresh fruit, Greek yogurt, and some granola. As I was slicing up the fruit, in walks Richard.

"Hello," I said to him, trying not to sound too nervous around him. Ever since I started investigating, being around him gave me the creeps. At first, I thought he was just overly private, but now he comes off as a sociopath with a secret. "Hello, Noelle, how are you and my granddaughter this afternoon?" he asked, sounding genuinely concerned. I relaxed a little and decided to engage him in conversation further. "we are ok. Just tired and sore" I responded as I took a bite of my food. It was good, but my appetite just wasn't there. "well that's good to hear. I was wondering when you were going to get up today" he replied looking at me with an intense look. I got the funny feeling that he knew I had been up to something. I just ignored my thoughts and replied, " yeah being pregnant definitely takes a lot out of you". He chuckled and went and poured himself some coffee. Maybe he didn't know anything and once again I was making a big deal out of nothing. I finished my food and washed out my dishes. I know that I didn't have to, but I still hadn't gotten used to having maids wait on me when I can just clean up behind myself. Just when I thought I could go back upstairs and stop worrying Richard called my name. "Noelle, can you come back for a second?" I walked slowly back into the kitchen, wondering what he could possibly have to say. "lovely day for gardening, isn't it?" he asked, looking at me with the most serious face I've ever seen him make. "umm sure?" I said nervously. Fidgeting with my hair. Wishing I was a thousand miles away. "maybe if you're up to it, we can pick out some roses and plant them for Summer Rose. That way when she gets here she can see the flowers we planted in her honor. I have the perfect spot for it. Right in the back by the oak trees. The soil has already been broken anyways" he said. Burning a hole into my eyes with his. He knew. He must have seen me last night when he was up in the private wing. That may be what he and the other person was arguing about. I had to think of what to say and quick. I felt sick to my stomach with fear. All I could muster to squeak out in the tiniest voice was, "I don't fee so good, but that is a lovely idea. Maybe another day when I am up to it". He softens his face just a smidge and puts on the fakest smile ever. " well feel better Noelle, and get some rest" he said. I backed away slowly and went back upstairs, locking the door behind me.

Today put things into perspective for me. Richard was not only crazy, but now I believe he's dangerous. I had to give Daniel the ultimatum. Me and Summer Rose or his parents. He was scheduled to get off house arrest in 5 days and on that day I wanted to be packed up and moving as far away as possible. I was approaching 6 months pregnant, and I couldn't afford to keep being as stressed as I am. My appetite is terrible, I'm acting out of character, I can barely focus on work, and I feel my sanity slipping away from me. This wasn't pregnancy brain. This was full-fledged fear and paranoia. Although I was sore, I decided to order dinner from our favorite Italian spot and break the news to him gently. I lit the candles and put on the lingerie. Hoping that it would make it that much harder to tell me no. He loved how I looked pregnant. He said I was the sexiest woman he's ever seen. When he came in the room from his shower, his face lit up from the sight of everything I prepared.

"Either you want something big, or I've been a very good boy," he said. Wrapping his arms around me and kissing my neck. I felt myself throb, but I wouldn't be deterred from my mission. I kissed him quickly and invited him to take a seat. "Actually there are some things I'd like to talk to you about," I said fixing his plate and pouring his wine. "what about?" he said taking a bite of a bread stick. "Well honey, I know Friday is the day you get off of house arrest, I found a wonderful house with lush gardens that we could buy. It's right outside of the city but close enough to my job and the shopping district. We could leave Friday evening, stay in a hotel, and be in the house within a week". Just then the happy look on his face disappeared, and was replaced by a look that resembled anger and fear at the same time. "what about the nursery here? What about my mom helping us out? I don't want some stranger caring for Summer Rose." He said, sounding like he was holding back a plethora of emotions. "I know how you feel Daniel, but I don't feel comfortable here. Something strange is going on, and you can act like you don't know, but I know that you do. You may be able to ignore it, or maybe you're used to it, however I will not raise my child in an environment like this." His face turned to pure anger with that statement. "Your child? So I guess I'm not her father anymore? It's not only up to you, and you are being unfair! We have everything we need here. More than you could ever ask for, why mess up a great situation?" He was livid. Almost to the verge of tears. I felt bad for saying my child instead of ours, but I needed him to understand my concerns. "I'm sorry baby. Summer is our daughter, and we do have a lot here. More money and space than we could ever need, but the one thing in don't have is a peace of mind. It can't be good for her being inside this hostile environment I call my body. I can't eat. I can't sleep. I can't focus. All I keep thinking about it that poor missing girl. And that stupid secret wing. I need to get away from here. I'd love for it to be with you, but understand I'm leaving Friday either way." I was crying at this point. All the emotions came over me like a flood. I could see him hurting for me. He hated to see me cry. The room went silent for what seemed like an eternity. Finally, he spoke up in the saddest voice I've ever heard. "If you feel so strongly that you would consider leaving me, then I have no choice but to leave too. I will not lose you two. My parents are the family I was born into and the only family I've ever known, but you are the family I've chosen. We have a baby on the way, and we are getting married. We'll break the news to them tomorrow morning. I just want you to be happy." He stood up, scooped me into his big strong arms and just held me. We cried together, but for very different reasons.

Chapter 9

I made eggs Benedict. I knew it was one of Richard's favorite meals so I thought it would be fitting to tell him our plans when he has a full stomach. I cut up some fresh fruit and poured some mimosas. Water for me of course. A little booze may lessen the blow as well. I took the food and set it out beautifully on the table overlooking the garden. I wanted everything to be perfect. This news wasn't going to be easy to break, so I wanted to create an environment where it would be almost impossible to be angry.

"You went through a lot of trouble to please my parents," Daniel said, grabbing the bowl of fruit from me and sitting it on the table. "I just wanted us to have one last meal together before we move out," I said to him, moving the bowl he sat down into the perfect position on the table. Just then Mary and Richard walked out and took a seat at the table. One of the maids followed behind to serve the meal. I wanted to interject and serve it myself, but I knew it would be best to sit next to Daniel and be a united front.

"This is simply amazing," Richard said, stuffing his face with the eggs Benedict. "What's the special occasion?" Mary asked, getting straight to the point. She never was the one for niceties. I grabbed Daniel's hand and looked at him for confirmation. He nodded and before I could talk, he blurted it all out.

"Noelle and I are moving out Friday. I'll be off house arrest, and although we love and appreciate all you have done, we think it would be best to raise Summer Rose in our own home." The look on Mary's face was perplexing. I didn't know whether she wanted to cry or kill us both. I interrupted the intense silence. " We would love for you to come visit and we'll bring her by often. We just need to build our family in our own space and do it our own way."

Still silence. This time the emotions were more easy to decipher. Mary was sad, but Richard was pissed. "After all we've done for you Daniel, you've never wanted for anything. You have the best education, the finest of clothing, you practically have the world at your disposal, and you tell me you are leaving? Just like that? You never wanted to leave until this negro came into your life and messed your head up! We raise our own in this house! Generations before me were born here, and I wanted it to be generations to come!" Richard said, so mad he was spitting. All I could think about is this asshole called me "this negro" like we were back on the plantation. Before I could let the ATL come out and check him, Daniel spoke up for me. "Don't you ever refer to my fiancé and mother of my child in that manner. I understand your displeasure, but she is part of the family. You don't have to agree with our decisions, but frankly, I don't give a damn. I am an adult, and it's time I get my freedom!" The way that he said that turned me on, but made me alarmed. The way he said his freedom made it seem like the option to leave was never possible before today. It was probably the way they smothered him so and how codependent they were before I came into the picture and gave him the desire to see more. To be more. My thoughts got interrupted by Mary's sobbing. "You have hurt me dearly Daniel. You know how I feel about you leaving here, but more importantly, you have upset your father. I thought we were past all of this rebellion and we could live here peacefully. I guess not. We allowed you to entertain this woman because you were growing lonely. Even welcomed her into our home. We even accepted the fact she got pregnant 3 minutes after arriving for the sake of keeping our family together. Better to welcome more people than to lose the ones that matter. We've bent over backwards, and you still decide to abandon us? I just don't understand," she said, fighting back tears and wiping her runny nose with her silk handkerchief.

All of this was just too weird for me. They were treating him like a little boy. He was a grown man and capable of making his own decisions. Daniel grabbed my hand again and snapped me out of my thoughts. He stood up and pulled me up with him. "We are leaving Friday evening. I hope that you can learn to respect our decisions for the sake of Summer Rose. I'd hate for her not to know her grandparents because of their unwillingness to change." He placed his hand on my back and guided me in the house and up the stairs to our room. I didn't know how to process what just happened. All I knew was that we were leaving Friday, and after everything that happened, it couldn't be soon enough.

We stayed in the room all day like we were on punishment or something. We both were trying to wait as long as possible before we had another interaction with the sob squad. The sun was starting to set, and my stomach was starting to growl. Right as I was getting ready to work up enough courage to go to the kitchen, we heard a knock on the door. It was his parents. They were looking like they were in better spirits than they were earlier. " We came up to apologize to you both and invite you to dinner to celebrate. We are traditionalists and realized we may be stuck in our ways. We have had a feast prepared in your honor."

I was elated! Thank God they came around to the idea. I was worried that the next couple of days would be awkward and miserable. I grabbed Daniel's hand to proceed to the dining room, but his face didn't look so relieved. He actually had a look of concern on his face. I told his parents we'd meet them down there in ten minutes and closed the door. I asked him what was wrong?

"My parents have never folded so easily. They could be dead wrong, and it would still take weeks before things got back to normal. Even then they wouldn't admit they were wrong, they'd just act as if nothing has ever happened and we'd move on". He was seriously worried. I figured I'd try to put his mind at ease a bit. "Well, baby, this time there is a lot more at stake. You weren't moving out or threatening to keep their first grandchild away from them. They knew they had to do something before we left." That seemed to help him relax a bit. That wrinkle he always got in the middle of his forehead softened, and I could almost make out a smile. "maybe you are right love, let's go down before they change their minds!" We giggled a bit and headed to the dining hall.

The spread was amazing. All of our favorite foods were on the table. Even a sweet potato pie I know was there just for me. They certainly went out of their way say they were sorry. I sat down and began eating right away. I was starving, and I know the baby needed nourishments too. I ate ox tails, fried chicken, macaroni and cheese, collard greens, deviled eggs, and washed it all down with peach sweet tea. It was delicious. I realized I hadn't come up for air I was eating so much, so I decided to take a break before dessert to make conversation.

"Everything was amazing," I said, wiping the food off of my face. "You really outdid yourself with this meal." Daniel, who had been scarfing the food down himself, chimed in to express his gratitude as well. " Mother, Father, I am so pleased that you've had a change of heart. Noelle and I love each other very much and can't wait to show you how great we will be as parents."

Richard raised his glass and asked to make a toast. "We are so happy to have Noelle as part of our family and can't wait for little Summer Rose to arrive as well. We understand you guys want your own space, so we want to give it to you. Just remember, you asked for this, so you shall receive!" He took a sip of his wine and Mary did the same. Although the toast was super weird, I decided to drink my tea so that I didn't offend them any further. I drank every drop. I looked up, and Daniel was still holding his glass. He looked horrified as if he had seen a ghost. He stood up and grabbed my hand. Before I could ask what was wrong, I was already on my feet moving quickly out the dining hall. I started to feel dizzy and disoriented. Like my tea may have had some liquor in it, but I knew it didn't. I could hear Daniel screaming and crying, but I couldn't make out what he was saying. All I heard was Noelle stay with me, we are going to get out of here. I tried to keep moving, but my legs gave out. I felt myself getting extremely tired. Daniel was hovering over me. The look in his eyes was one I've never seen. I tried to ask what was going on, but my body gave in to exhaustion. I closed my eyes. Everything went quiet.

Chapter 10

My head feels like I've been hit with a ton of bricks. The room is dark, and they have me tied up in ropes. I'd scream for help, but my mouth is taped shut. I thought this crap only happened in movies. I always knew some weird stuff was going on, I just never thought I'd be victim to it.

Just then I felt summer kick. Thank God she's ok. They must have given me some type of tranquilizer, and I was scared it would affect her. There's some creepy classical music playing in the background. I had to figure out how to get free, but how? I started wriggling around to see if I could slip the cuffs. Just then, I heard the door begin to open.

It was Richard. Dressed up in a lab coat and latex gloves. He looked as though he was about to perform surgery and I just prayed I wasn't the patient. I hadn't been a religious person most of my life, but I needed God more than ever. He interrupted my prayers to talk to me. "I tried to work with you, Noelle. My whole instincts told me not to allow you to come, but I felt he earned a companion. He assured me you'd be different than the last. That you would appreciate just being here, but he was wrong. You are all the same. You just happened to be the only one to get pregnant."

"What did he mean? Different than the last?" I tried to talk, but with the tape over my mouth, it was just mumbles. He snatched the tape off so hard it felt as if he took part of my face with it. "Speak up little girl, I can't hear you," he said in a taunting way. He was enjoying this. I wanted to hit him. But the ropes around my wrists were so tight it was rubbing my skin off. I was captive. I decided I better do and say what he wanted , because who knows what else he's capable of. I saw the body being hurried, I didn't want to meet the same fate.

"Why are you doing this to me?" I managed to say through my tears. I was scared. Not just for me but for the baby. I was worried about Daniel too. I didn't know where he was, or what happened to him. " What did you do to Daniel? We don't deserve this" I said, still hyperventilating. "Daniel is back in the quiet room. He clearly has forgotten how to behave, so I have to do a little reprogramming" " He doesn't know how to behave? He's a grown man! He's your son! How could you treat human beings this way?" I was able to say that more clearly. The fear I felt was being overshadowed by anger. I know I needed to tread lightly, but my blood was boiling. "Noelle, you just don't get it. Let me tell you a little story, and maybe then you'll understand everything.

"Once upon a time, there was a man and a woman. They loved each other dearly, so they decided to get married. When the time came to start a family, they tried and tried with no success. They had 3 miscarriages, and 1 stillbirth. Finally, the doctor dealt the final blow. The woman needed to have her uterus removed due to cancer. She would bare no children. They tried to go on and live their lives, but something was missing. They had all this money, but nobody to love and share it with. One day a pregnant woman came looking for work. She said she had nowhere to go and would work for room and board for her and her unborn child. The couple agreed to take her in. After her baby was born the woman of the house would spend a lot of time with the worker. She became so obsessed with the little baby she decided to make the worker a generous offer. She would give her enough money to live comfortably for the rest of her days, as long as she gave up the baby and moved far away. The woman refused. She continued to live in the house, and the woman of the house became more desperate. The man of the house hated to see his wife unhappy, so he decided something had to be done. He invited the woman to dinner, much like the one we had tonight, but instead of putting her to sleep temporarily, he gave her something a bit more permanent. They disposed of the body, and they finally had the child they always wanted. They raised him as their own, but the guilt of what happened got to the both of them. They had feared that someone would come and take him away. They became mad with fear. So mad they decided he could never leave the house. At first, it worked out fine, but as the boy free older he became more curious with the world. The gardens and all the land wasn't enough to cure his curiosity. He had the best of everything, clothes, toys, food, teachers, but all he wanted was freedom. One day the couple caught the boy trying to run away. They put him in a quiet room so he could think about what he did. He'd stay in there for weeks at a time whenever he tried to leave. As he got older, he realized he couldn't go anywhere, so he decided to ask his parents for a friend. They thought long and hard, but decided it was a doable request. They let him out of his quiet room and placed an electronic monitor on his ankle. He could have a friend if he'd liked, but if the monitor ever went off, it was back in the quiet room he went. Soon, the quiet room became a quiet wing. A secret one where all of Daniel's friends would be kept. Eventually, the man began collecting his own friends as well. The woman of the house knew what was going on, but as long as she had her son, nothing else mattered." He stood up and walked closer to me. So close that I could feel his hot breath on my face. "You see Noelle, everything was finally perfect. Until the son became involved with a woman online. He didn't want a friend to be forced to be here. He wanted love. He wanted to be chosen. Despite our concerns, we allowed that to happen. Dozens of friends came, and dozens of friends died, including the girl Elizabeth you asked about. He no longer wanted me to get him his friends. I agreed on the terms that he never left as we had agreed before. I continued to collect my own treasures, but he was free to find his own. That's when he found you. You made him fall in love. He had you come here so he could be with you, but he still knew he was never to leave. You placed all of this foolishness in his head. You got pregnant. Now he's back to the little boy we have to lock up. Now we have to lock up his friends again too. I'll be back in the morning to check on you. Just know, you brought this on yourself." He placed the tape back on my mouth. Turned up the weird music, and left out the room. I heard the door lock behind him. I couldn't believe what he just said. Everything I thought I knew was a lie. Daniel wasn't on house arrest. He was a prisoner. He wasn't even their son. I had to get the hell out of this place. I needed to find a way to escape. I just didn't know how. I laid down on the mat on the floor. I was still drowsy from the meds. I decided to try to get some rest and figure it out tomorrow. I'd need all my strength for whatever was to come.

Chapter 11

I'm either going to have to kill him, or kill him with kindness. I can't get free from these ropes no matter how hard I try. I am sore all over. Being this pregnant and sleeping on a thin mat just doesn't mix. I haven't bathed in 3 days. I smell of sweat and desperation. I could've had a shower, but I refuse to let them undress me. They can take away my freedom, but my dignity was all I have left. Luckily I have a plan. The biggest threat is the fear of losing Daniel. I had to convince them that I no longer wanted to leave. If I said I would just go, they'd kill me. They weren't going to risk this secret getting out. Just thinking about how many bodies were buried under the trees sent a cold chill down my spine.

As I was gathering my thoughts I heard the ever familiar footsteps coming down the hall. I had to get into character. My life depended on it. Richard walked in and sat down in a chair right in front of me. He leaned in as if he was going to kiss me, but instead he ripped the tape off of my mouth. "Hello Noelle. Are you feeling any better since yesterday? I figured I'd give you some time to calm down and come to your senses." I felt sick to my stomach at the sight of him. I took a deep breath and swallowed my emotions. " I feel much more at peace today. I realized I was acting unstable and I apologize. These hormones from this pregnancy have really gotten the best of me. All you have done is showed me love and hospitality. You've allowed me to join your son, in your home, and all I've done is caused problems. I understand why you had to bring me in here. I have seen the error of my ways." I took a hard swallow. I almost threw up in my mouth after spewing all of those lies. I managed to fake a smile. I tried to be as convincing as I humanly could. Richard's face softened. He actually looked pleased. "See, I knew all you needed was some time. Mary told me to just kill you, but I knew you would come to your senses. We are so happy to welcome a new baby here. We haven't had one since

Daniel was a baby himself. If you can follow our rules and stop these foolish ideas of leaving, you're more than welcome to live here with all of us. If not, well I'd hate to keep you down here until the baby is born. I'd hate even more for Summer to be raised without her mother. She is half Daniel, therefore, she belongs to the Seymour family. She will be raised here." He stood up, walked over to me and kissed me long and hard on my lips. Every muscle in my body cringed with anger, but I quickly made sure it didn't show on my face. Instead, I looked at him in his eyes and smiled. I leaned in and kissed him again. This time passionately. I slid my tongue in his mouth. It was hot and tasted of old scotch. He wrapped his arms around me and grabbed my behind. He took his other hand and stroked my hair. I gently pulled away and sat in the chair. " I don't want to leave my family. I don't want to leave you Richard" I licked my lips and bit my lip while staring at him sensually. He adjusted his package, straightened out his tie, and wiped the corners of his mouth. "I'm so glad to have you here Noelle. It seems like we are going to get along just fine!" He left reached for the tape, then changed his mind. " I don't think we need this anymore. I'll send one of the maids down with fresh clothes and a wash basin. A beautiful woman such as yourself should look and smell accordingly." He walked out the door and locked it behind himself. I waited until I heard the footsteps disappear then ran over to the bucket in the corner. I threw up until nothing else would come out. I was repulsed, but I was alive, and one step closer to my freedom.

About an hour later, just as Richard said, 2 of the maids came in lugging a portable tub behind them. It was filled with hot water and sweet smelling bubble bath. I didn't want to give in, but I needed to soak my aching body. Plus the smell of my own body was making me sick. I allowed them to undress me and wash my body. They washed my hair and dressed me in a fresh gown. They brushed my teeth and put my hair in a bun. "Master Richard picked out this gown himself," said one maid. They sprayed me with my favorite perfume and wheeled out the tub. Right as they walked out one of the butlers walked in and removed the mat. He brought in a bed with the little wheels on the bottom. He made it up with beautiful linens and plenty of pillows. "Master Richard told me to tell you this is what being a good girl gets you. You may also pick whatever you'd like to eat for dinner." I made my mind up quickly. " I want a nice juicy steak and baked potato," I said to him. I was praying when they brought it to me, they brought the steak knife as well. "Right away Ms. Jones," he said. He walked out and locked the door behind him. I laid down on the bed. I felt clean and smelled wonderful. It was so soft warm in comparison to the mat I was just sleeping on last night. I smiled to myself and closed my eyes. Everything was working out exactly the way I wanted. I allowed myself to drift off. This was going To be the best sleep I've had since I laid in Daniel's arms.

I woke up to the savory aroma of a juicy steak. My stomach growled and my mouth watered. Since I've been locked up, all I have eaten is bread and water. They were punishing me, but the made sure I got prenatal vitamins daily. I didn't realize just how hungry I was. I sat up in bed and adjusted my eyes. On the other side of the room was a beautiful spread of delectable goodies. Steak, carmalized onions and mushrooms, baked potatoes, salad, dinner rolls with real butter, and sweet potato pie. They also had a pitcher of lemonade. However, I wasn't so keen on the idea of drinking anything with the seal already broken. I walked over and sat at the table. I noticed they had real silverware on the table. Forks and knives. I waited on one of the butlers to come in and untie me. I planned on tucking a knife into my panties whenever they weren't looking. Instead, in walks Richard. He took a blade and cut my ropes free. I almost lunged at him, but I realized I didn't know exactly how to escape or if there were any guards outside the door. I decided to play it cool. He pushed my chair in and proceeded to the other side of the table. He grabbed a plate and started fixing it for me. He sat it down in front of me and made a plate for himself. He took a seat and looked at me with lustful eyes. "You look and smell magnificent," he said, sounding as if he was still aroused from our embrace earlier that day. I managed to put on a smile and said thank you. "Well, aren't you going to eat? I had the chef prepare everything you asked for and then some he said" looking at me with concern. I looked at all the food but was nervous to eat any of it. He picked up his fork and took a bite of everything on the table and washed it down with a sip of lemonade as if he could read my mind. I began to eat the food feverishly. It was probably the best steak I had ever had, or at least my hunger was making me believe it was.

" I really enjoyed our kids Noelle. It woke up a part of me that I didn't know still existed. The fire I felt for Mary has long died out. Don't get me wrong, I love her, but the attraction is no longer there." He loosened up his tie and Tossled his hair a bit, trying to appear a bit more relaxed. I decided to play into his lust for me. It may just be the quickest way out of this prison. " I enjoyed it too Richard. I can't deny I'm attracted to you. You are so strong and powerful. Daniel is wonderful, but he is weak. I need a real man to guide my steps" I unbuttoned my top three buttons to my gown, exposing my plump breasts. I didn't have on a bra, and since they were engorged from the pregnancy, the sat up nice like they were ready to be tasted. I took my hair down and shook it freely, just like Daniel liked for me to do. I took a dollop of whipped cream off my pie and sucked my finger while staring deeply into his eyes. He cleared his throats as if the very sight of me was choking him. He spoke again, but this time his voice was deeper and more seductive. I could tell I had his full attention. "I love my son too. You are carrying his child. Part of me feels so bad for even looking at you in such a manner, but I am a man. You are very beautiful. I have been secretly captivated by your beauty ever since you have arrived. It's partially the reason why I didn't end the defiance sooner. I know you've been spying on me. There is a camera right outside the entrance of the wing. Every night that you've listened at the door, I have seen you. I've also seen the way you make love to my son. Now there are no cameras in your bedroom, I agreed not to do that with Daniel long before you arrived. However, there are cameras overlooking the garden. I saw the night you two made love by the flowers. So sensual and free. You had no inhibitions. You took him into your mouth, and I saw his soul leave his body. Then you climbed on top of him and rode him into the sunset. I felt bad for watching, but even worse for the amount of times I've replayed the video. I've pleasured myself while watching, but I never thought I'd have the opportunity to actually experience it." He stood up and walked to the door. He told the guards to go ahead and leave, then he walked over to me. His shaft was presenting through his slacks. I didn't want him to touch me, but I knew that was the only chance I would have to escape. He swept my hair from my neck and began to kiss on it. His mustache tickled my neck while his tongue slid all over it like some sort of serpent. He stood me up from my chair and placed his hands on my breasts. He removed my gown from my shoulders exposing all that they had to offer. He took my hard nipple into his mouth and sucked as if he wanted to be fed. He sucked one and then the other. I tried so hard not to get stimulated however my body has a mind of its own. I began to throb down there, and it made my stomach turn. If I was going to make it through this ordeal, I was going to have to travel somewhere else in my mind. I thought of the first time Daniel and I made love, I began to moan quietly. He took his hand and slid it up my gown. He let out a deep groan when he felt how wet I had gotten. He rubbed my pearl vigorously while sucking on my breast. I didn't want to enjoy it, but it felt so good. Before I knew it was orgasming repeatedly. My legs got weak and started to shake. I almost collapsed, but he grabbed my wrists and pulled me up. I jumped from the pain caused my the rope burns on my wrists. He looked ashamed at the marks and kissed them both. He licked his fingers that he pleasured me with then kissed me deeply. I could taste my sweet juice all over his tongue. This time I didn't mind his mouth so much. He pulled out his penis and sat me on the bed. I took him into my mouth and sucked him the way that I did Daniel. He was moaning and shaking and rubbing his hands through my hair. Before I could decide whether I should just bite him or not, his warm fluids flowed into my mouth. I swallowed it and thought quickly. I threw him down onto the bed and got on top of him. Although he was a much older man, his libido was still strong. He had ejaculated, but he was still ready to go. I slid him inside of me and began to ride him. I had him exactly where I wanted him. I stopped before he could cum again and told him I wanted to play a game. Anxious to continue he agreed. I tied up his hands to the rails of the bed. Then I tied up his feet. I climbed back on top to make him believe I just wanted to dominate him I let him finish inside of me. He was panting heavily, and extremely exhausted. I hopped up, grabbed the tape, and placed it over his mouth. He began kicking and trying to get his arms free. I had tied them too tightly for it to work. I got dressed and got the keys out of his pants pockets. I walked to his side and kissed him on the cheek. I whispered, "be a good boy for mommy" to him and walked out the room, locking the door behind me.

Chapter 12

I tiptoed down the long hallway. The wooden floors creaked under the weight of my body, so I made sure to apply as little pressure as possible. The halls were dark except for a dim light coming from a room a few doors down. I quickly walked over to the door, so I could look inside and see what the glow was.

Inside was what appeared to be a control room. There were computer monitors everywhere and other equipment used to monitor the whole estate. I slowly turned the knob to see if it was open. I knew the guards were long gone due to Richard's desire to have me to himself with no witnesses. The doorknob clicked and slowly opened up. I slowly slid inside and closed the door quietly behind me.

I was taken aback my the amount of rooms displayed on the screens. The hallways, bedrooms, kitchen, garden, indoor theater, and pool all had surveillance cameras watching every second of the day. I noticed that right by the door to the secret wing, it was indeed a camera overlooking it just as Richard had said. All of those days that I thought I was sneaking around trying to find some evidence, he had been one step ahead of me. No wonder the body wasn't there when I dug up the spot behind the tree. There was a camera pointing over that exact spot.

I looked on the next wall of monitors and noticed a bunch of rooms I didn't recognize. They all looked similar to the room Richard was keeping me in for the last three days. Then I saw on the third monitor from the bottom, Richard lying helplessly on the bed. He was naked and shivering. I got a huge feeling of satisfaction seeing him so vulnerable. Now he knew exactly how I felt. How all of the ones before me felt. I scanned the monitors for the room Daniel had to be locked in. I couldn't find him in any of them. I got a sick feeling in the pit of my stomach that something may have happened to him. I did, however, find 4 separate monitors with other people held captive in different rooms.

In the first room, there was a young girl. She looked to be no more than sixteen years old. She was dressed in appeared to be a doll costume. Her hair was in 2 pigtails. She had makeup on her porcelain colored skin. Dark pink blush and a red lip. There were toys everywhere for her to play with. She looked so defeated sitting on that bed. Saw a button that looked as if it controlled the sound volume to the monitors. I cut it up just a little, so I could hear what was going on inside the rooms.

The same creepy classical music was playing that almost drove me insane. Day in and day out, no relief from the noise. I looked closer at the girl, and I could see that her makeup was smudged from the tears that she had been crying. I felt my eyes fill up with tears as well. There's no telling how long she had been kept locked away in that prison. In another room was one of the maids I hadn't seen in a while. It was Florence. She was always so nice to me and would warn me that I needed to get out while I still had the chance. I couldn't help but feel that it must've been because of me that she was locked away. Richard must've found footage of her warning me. That it wasn't safe to live here. She was weeping quietly, still dressed up in her maids uniform. Her hair was disheveled, and she had something else playing in the background. It was Richards voice reading off what sounded like the rules of the house. In the third room was a little boy. He looked a lot like Daniel. His room was much nicer than the rest of prisons he kept us in. He was playing with toys and had a table of cakes and cookies at his disposal. I couldn't help but think, they were grooming him to replace Daniel since I couldn't seem to find Daniel in any of the secret rooms.

The last room had an elderly lady rocking in a rocking chair knitting what looked like a baby blanket. It was a beautiful pink color with a lavender S in the middle of it. The S must've stood for Summer Rose. The woman looked so familiar to me. I looked at her face a few more seconds before I realized it was Richard's mother! I had seen her picture hanging in one of the hallways, and he told me that she had passed away a few years earlier. That she had died peacefully in her sleep. He was so sick that he locked his own mother away in order to have complete dominion over his kingdom. I had seen enough. I went back to the other screens to look and see if any of them were guarded. There was nobody in sight. I headed towards the door until a monitor caught my eye . It was surveillance of our bedroom door. It just opened up, and to my shock,

Daniel strolled out and headed down the hallway. He wasn't dead or being held captive in some room being tortured. He was free to roam about the house as if nothing had happened at all. I watched him go into the kitchen and fix himself a sandwich. Mary entered in and gave him a kiss on the cheek. I turned up the volume to the kitchen monitor. I had to hear what the hell he had to say to her.

"Good evening Daniel, how are you feeling?" She asked him in the most loving and concerned tone. "I'm ok, mother, about as good as could be expected. I just don't understand what is taking so long for father to release Noelle. Surely she has learned her lesson and is ready to join the family again." I heard his voice crack as if he were fighting back tears as he spoke about me. "You know your father does things on his own timing dear. If she was ready, she'd be released by now. Just have patience." She said to him as she poured herself a cup of milk. She rubbed his shoulder and left out the kitchen. A few seconds later Daniel threw his plate across the room, and it broke into a bunch of little pieces all over the floor. He fell to his knees and sobbed uncontrollably. He was clearly heartbroken at what was going on with me. "I'm so sorry Noelle! I have failed you. I have failed our child. We should've just left when we had the chance" He said out loud as if he thought I might be able to hear him. In walked one of the butlers who literally stepped over Daniel and swept up the mess he made. He finally stood up off the floor and slowly walked back to our room. Richard told the truth when he said there was no camera in our room. I wish there had been at that moment. My heart broke for Daniel. Although I was being held captive in that hell hole. He has been held captive all of his life. He couldn't possibly be held responsible for everything that was going on. He needed someone to break him free just as much as I did. It was going to be much harder with him, however, because he was not only physically stuck here but mentally he was prisoner as well. Just to think that he's never stepped foot outside of this estate was enough to make me sick to my stomach. I ran over to the trash can in the corner and threw up again. I emptied myself of all the steak, all of the fluid Richard shot down my throat, all of my misery, and all of my weakness. Once I was finished, I felt empty inside. Numb to everything except one feeling, rage. I was going to get my family out of here tonight. Daniel and I were going to be together and raise our child. Richard and Mary were going to pay for what they have done to so many innocent people through the years. I was going to free the other prisoners being kept like a part of his collection of acquired things. This was all going to come to an end, or I was going to die trying. I left out the security room, tiptoed down the hall, And unlocked the door to the secret wing. I locked it behind me and walked towards my bedroom. I needed help to pull this off. I had to pay my fiancé a visit.

Chapter 13

I crept up the stairs to my bedroom door and entered it quickly. Daniel, who had been laying down sobbing quietly jumped up at the sound of the door open. He ran over and scooped me up into his arms and gave me the biggest hug ever. "Noelle, you are finally free!" He exclaimed. Looking as if all his prayers had been answered. I was so happy to be in his arms again as well; but I couldn't deter from my mission. "Put me down, Daniel. We have a lot to discuss and quickly." I said to him, pushing myself away from him and struggling to break free from our embrace. He put me down, looking perplexed like he didn't understand why I wasn't as happy to see him as he was to see me. I grabbed his hand and guided him to the bed. I sat down and pulled him down next to me. " Richard didn't let me go. I escaped. He told me everything. I know you aren't on house arrest. I know you're not their son. I know you've never been outside the gate. Why didn't you tell me the truth from the beginning?" He grabbed my hand and tears began running down his face. He quickly wiped them away as if he didn't want me to see him so vulnerable.

" I knew you would never talk to me if you knew the truth. From the moment I saw your picture, I knew you would be my wife. I got to know you, and for the first time, I saw a life outside of these walls. I thought that if my parents could see how much happier I was with you, they'd finally let me go. Once I knew they still wanted me to stay, I decided to convince them to let you stay too. You kept looking into everything, you wouldn't let the secrets go.

The more you looked, the angrier Father became. He told me if I didn't allow him to fix you, the way they fixed me, he would kill you once Summer Rose was born. I agreed to let him, but changed my mind. The day you were drugged I had no clue that he would take matters into his own hands so soon. I thought I had time to convince him to let us go. The monitor on my ankle is real. It tracks my every move. If we are going to get out of here, we'll have to get rid of it somehow. It sounds an alarm in the control room whenever I stray too far." Just then I had a plan. It was risky, but it was the only way we would be free. I finished telling him of the torture I endured, and how Richard came on to me. I told him how I had to have sex with him just to catch him off guard and escape. He became enraged at the thought of him touching me. It seemed to be exactly what he needed to make him ready to escape.

I went outside and walked around to the circuit breaker box. I broke it open with a screwdriver and cut off the main power source to the house. I knew that the backup generator wasn't working because it had stormed no too long ago, and when the power went out it never cut on. We had to light candles until the power was restored. I ran back inside, and Daniel and I went back to the secret wing. We went inside and headed over to the control room. Daniel took a hammer and smashed all of the equipment to dust. He cut the ankle bracelet off and we headed towards the entrance. He asked me to show him the room I was being kept in. I showed him the door, so he can see how I humiliated Richard. We looked inside, but to our surprise, he was no longer there! He grabbed my hand, and we ran to the door. As I ran out in front of him, I heard a crash behind me. I spun around and saw Daniel lying on the floor. Mary had hit him in the head with one of her glass figurines. Before I could run away, I felt someone grab me from behind. The smell of his breath let me know it was Richard. I struggled to get free. I was not going down without a fight. He placed his hand over my mouth from behind. I bit down so hard I tasted his blood on my tongue. He let out a high pitched scream and quickly let me go. I picked up a vase and hit him in the head with it. He collapsed onto the floor. Mary, who looked like she saw the devil himself was backing away from Daniel and down the hall. I was so angry. I lunged at her and brought her to the floor. She placed her hands in front of her face in order to shield the blows. I just punched her repeatedly in the stomach instead. Once she grabbed her stomach from all the pain, she felt I punched her as hard as I could in her face. I hit her over and over and over again. I felt my finger break from the impact, but I didn't care. I hit her until her face was unrecognizable from all the blood. Once

I snapped out of my rage and realized she was unconscious, I got up to go help, Daniel. He was struggling to get to his feet, and the back of his head was bleeding. I gave him my hand and helped him up. I took his shirt off of him and tied it around his head to stop the bleeding. When we went to finish off Richard, we saw that he was missing. Somehow throughout the fight with Mary, he manage to escape. We dragged Mary to a closet and locked her inside. I told him we needed to go and grabbed his hand to lead him to the door. He snatched it away from me and refused to budge. "I need to find Richard," he said in a voice I had never heard before from him. He sounded possessed with anger. He was not leaving without finishing what I had started. I grabbed my phone and called the police. I told them to come someone was trying to kill us and hung up. There was a trail of blood leading out the patio door from the kitchen. We grabbed some knives and followed the drops to the shed.

We entered quietly and followed the trail to a table. On top of it was an opened box. Daniel's face filled with worry. "This is the box where the groundskeeper keeps the guns," he said, slowly backing up towards the door. Just as we were about to leave out, Richard appeared from behind a shelf and pointed the gun straight at us.

"Step away from the door and put your hands in the air," he said aiming the gun from me to Daniel, and back to me again. We backed away from the door and placed our hands in the air. Daniel looked at me as if to apologize for everything I had gone through since I've arrived. A single tear ran down his cheek. My eyes filled up with tears as well, but I refuse to let Richard see me cry ever again. "Just let Noelle go, and I'll stay here," Daniel said slowly stepping towards the barrel of the gun. Richard cocked it and instructed Daniel to stop in his tracks. While his gaze was fixed on Daniel, I slowly inched away from the two of them. I wanted to put enough space between us where he had to choose between shooting one or the other. Out of the corner of my eye, I saw another shotgun in the corner of the shed.

"Daniel, my sweet boy, I don't know why you think you are in a position to make requests at this point. I have spent your whole life, trying to find ways to make you happy. All the toys you had, all the friends I collected for you. You wanted for nothing, yet you were still an ungrateful bastard. You let this whore come in and destroy everything your mother and I worked so hard to build for us. I had the pleasure of experiencing her, and even though she's a good lay, it's not worth everything you have allowed her to ruin. Daniel's face went from scared to angry. His jaw was clenched so tightly, I thought it may break from the pressure. He looked at me and noticed what I was inching towards. He slowly began to walk in the opposite direction in order to get Richard to turn his back away from me.

"You are not my father! Mary is not my mother! My mother was killed a long time ago because you weren't man enough to give your wife a child." Slowly he stepped and slowly Richard turned away from me. "Your mother couldn't have children. I knew she could never get pregnant so I gave her the next best thing. How dare you speak on my manhood and you allowed me to screw your fiancé while you were barricaded in your room like some child. I poured myself into her, and she finally knew what a real man tasted like. Now you will both die all because you couldn't train your bitch to stay on a leash. I knew you were weak. That is why I have another little boy in my wing just waiting to take your place." I was finally far enough out of Richard's view I grabbed the shotgun and aimed it at the back of his head.

"Drop the gun, Richard!" I said pushing the barrel against the wound on his head that I caused when I hit him with the vase. He dropped the gun and placed his hands in the air. Daniel reached down and grabbed the gun. He then punched Richard dead in his face. "Sorry Richard, guess my bitch got off her leash again," Daniel said watching him stagger from the blow to the face. He aimed the other gun directly at Richard's forehead and instructed me to step out from behind him. I walked to the door and reminded Daniel the police were on the way. "Daniel, you don't have to kill him. The police will lock him and Mary up for the rest of their lives and every day they'll suffer and know what it's like to lose their freedom." I placed my hand on his shoulder, and I felt his body soften. He took the gun and struck Richard across the head. He collapsed onto the floor. We left out the shed and locked it behind us. We staggered towards the gate, but right before we could leave out, Mary shot in our direction. "Don't take another step. Nobody is leaving here alive" she said, pointing the gun in our direction. I lifted my gun and pointed it back at her. She began to walk closer to us, limping from all the damage I had caused her. Just then all of the maids and butlers came out of their quarters. They surrounded the three of us with guns, knives, bats, and other various weapons. We weren't going to make it out alive. I felt my legs almost give out from exhaustion. "You See Noelle I provide a good life here. Anything you wanted could have been yours. All you had to do was be grateful and stay put. We allowed you to go to work, and even when u were snooping around, we spared your life. Now you and Daniel can be together in death." She instructed the workers to grab us. Nobody moved. I decided I needed to speak up before they changed their minds.

"It's a shame what happened to Florence. Locked in a room, no windows, no hope. All because she disobeyed the rules of the house. She has on the same clothes she disappeared in, wallowing in her own filth. She was sobbing uncontrollably while Richard's voice played the rules over and over again . Don't ask questions you don't want the answer to huh? You guys are not staff members. You are prisoners, just like Daniel, and just like Florence. Don't you want to be free?" I looked around at all of them trying to read their expressions. William, the one who I saw hurrying the body, stepped in front towards the three of us. "Florence is my wife. You told me she left me and even gave me a dear John letter. I am no longer going to sit by and allow you to control us." He took a step closer to

Mary. She pointed the gun from us to him. It was now or never.

I cocked the shotgun and aimed it at her hand. I pulled the trigger, and the kickback knocked me to the ground. I looked up and saw Mary standing there. She had the look of horror on her face. He hand was on the ground, and all that was left was a bloody wrist. The staff started to walk around her. They got closer and closer. She begged and pleaded for her life, but nobody was willing to listen. Just as they grabbed her, the police showed up to the entrance. They had made it past the guards and the gates and arrived in the nick of time. They drew their weapons and instructed Daniel and the staff to drop their's as well. Daniel dropped his gun, and we put our hands in the air. They opened the gate and instructed us to walk out slowly. For the first time ever, Daniel took a step out of the Gateway. We were handcuffed and led away quickly to go and give a statement about what happened. They placed us in the back of a squad car together and was told by the captain to take us to the station. As we pulled off and out of the confinement of the property lines, we let out a sigh of relief. We were free. Even in the back of the police car we felt freer than we ever felt. Daniel sobbed with happiness. " This is the best day of my life," he said. He leaned it and kissed me, and we rode all the way to the station in silence.

The new beginning

"She's so beautiful," Daniel said as he gazed into Summer Rose's face while he laid her in her bassinet. She was seven months old and the perfect combination of the two of us. She had my curly locks and his beautiful blue eyes. We closed the door quietly and walked out onto our balcony to watch the sunset. We had finally finished unpacking and getting settled into our new place. We just purchased a beautiful pied-à-terre in the south of France.

The police had finished up their investigation, and all of the prisoners had been compensated for their suffering. They found a total of 27 different bodies buried throughout the property. The staff had all the charges dropped against them after they agreed to testify against the Seymours. Because of their age and and their status and wealth they were offered a plea deal to serve the rest of their lives in prison in order to avoid the death penalty. They gladly accepted it. The staff was given five years of severance pay, and the house was torn down and leveled off. It was the biggest headline in the history of England. Daniel and I sued the Seymours and were awarded fifty billion dollars. I stepped down from my position at the company and Angie replaced me as CEO. We took some of the money and gave back to all the families affected by the actions of Richard and Mary. We had a beautiful small ceremony in Cannes with just Angie, her family, Summer Rose, and Simba. We decided we'd spend the rest of our lives traveling the world. We never wanted to be tied down to anything except each other. We sat down and poured us a glass of wine. " I want to thank you for everything you have given me Noelle. Love, family, and freedom." We picked up our glasses and cheers to his statement. We sipped our wine and watched the sunset over the horizon. Love had turned to misery, and back to love again, but I finally got my happy ending.

The dedication

I know normally you find the dedication at the beginning of the book, but I wanted to switch things up...I dedicate this book to the most influential woman I've ever had the privilege to know. She lived a tough life, and died a tough death. She struggled to be the best person she knew how to be and I find myself doing the same thing. Just doing the best I know how to do. I just wanted to do something to honor her, and show her that sometimes, at the end of it all...We do win!

Love you Crystal Yvette Jarrett A.K.A Mommy

www.ingramcontent.com/pod-product-compliance
Lightning Source LLC
LaVergne TN
LVHW021300200225
804170LV00008B/375